Legs

Written by
Stephen Rickard

Two four six eight.
What has two legs?

A duck has two legs.
It walks and it swims
with its two legs.

Two four six eight.
What has four legs?

Look at this dog.
It has four legs.
It walks and it runs
and it plays
on its four legs.

Two four six eight.
What has six legs?

An ant has six legs.
It has long feelers too.
What does it do
with its legs?

Two four six eight.
What has eight legs?

A spider walks and jumps
and spins its web
with its eight legs.

Two four six eight.
What has more than
eight legs?

A centipede has
more than eight legs.
A centipede has
lots of legs.
It runs
fast on

Two

Four

Six

Eight

Lots!